THE CHIEF'S BLANKET

Michael Chanin

illustrated by
Kim Howard

H J Kramer
Starseed Press
Tiburon, CA

H J Kramer Inc
P.O. Box 1082
Tiburon, CA 94920

Library of Congress Cataloging-in-Publication Data

Chanin, Michael.
    The chief's blanket / by Michael Chanin ; illustrated by Kim
Howard.
        p.   cm.
    Summary: In the process of weaving her first Chief's Blanket,
Flower After the Rain discovers the meaning of giving and receiving.
    ISBN 0-915811-78-2
    1. Navajo Indians—Juvenile fiction. [1. Navajo Indians—
Fiction. 2. Indians of North America—Southwest, New—Fiction.
3. Weaving—Fiction.] I. Howard, Kim, ill. II. Title.
PZ7.C35969Ch   1998
[Fic]—dc21   97–7809
                                                                              CIP
                                                                              AC

Art Director: Linda Kramer
Editor: Nancy Grimley Carleton
Composition: Classic Typography
Printed in Hong Kong.
10 9 8 7 6 5 4 3 2 1

To my wife, Kim, who
has taught me to see the
world with eyes of wonder,
and to the memory of my
father, William Chanin.
M. C.

In memory of my grandparents,
Ruby and Vernon Clover,
who taught me discipline
and showed me the wonder of the sea.
K. H.

Once, at the foot of a mesa, there lived an old Navajo woman named Mockingbird Song. She was a weaver. She had a granddaughter whose name was Flower After the Rain, and the two lived in the country of the red rock tending sheep and weaving blankets made from their wool.

Often they would sit on the hot desert sands busy at their looms, and the girl would say, "Grandmother Mockingbird Song, please tell me again about the chiefs who live in the north country."

"Granddaughter," the old woman would begin, "there are chiefs who live far away in a land very different from ours—a land of great plains and flowing grasses. And throughout my life, child, these chiefs have visited me in our desert home. 'Mockingbird Song,' one of them would say, 'when the frigid north winds blow, my home is covered with ice and snow. Make me a blanket that will keep my family warm.'

"Granddaughter, these old, tired hands have made many blankets for the chiefs from the north country. It is an honor to weave a blanket for a chief, and my heart sings whenever I make one. But," Mockingbird Song added sadly, "I haven't seen a chief in many moons."

Flower After the Rain longed for the day when
a great chief and his people would come calling
on her beloved grandmother. The girl often gazed
toward the northern horizon, hoping to see signs of
their approach.

One day, when the old woman and the girl were busy preparing wool, Flower After the Rain looked out into the beautiful desert. She saw crows playing in the wind. She saw one of her people, Pinto Horse Man, grazing his horses. Suddenly, there was movement in the distance. The girl jumped up, pointed to the north horizon, and shouted, "Look, Grandmother, the winds bring strangers our way. Come look."

As she listened, Mockingbird Song heard familiar sounds and said, "Ho, granddaughter, the winds blow people our way. But these people are not strangers. A chief comes from the north country."

When the chief and his people first arrived, Mockingbird Song honored him with a small bundle of herbs. After this gesture of respect, the two elders sat on the ground in front of the looms and discussed the trade.

Mockingbird Song was not only known as a great weaver, but she was also considered a very skillful trader. The two talked in the chief's language, using their hands and making gestures that confused the girl. Flower After the Rain noticed that they kept glancing at her blanket.

Like a desert storm that is here one minute and gone the next, the chief and his people left as quickly as they had arrived. Mockingbird Song was laughing a thunderous laugh as they rode out of sight. Excitedly, Flower After the Rain asked, "Grandmother, what did the chief say? You are grinning so! Is he coming back to trade for one of your blankets?"

"Yes, he will be back before winter to trade for a blanket," said the old woman. "But not for one of mine. The chief admired your work and wants one of your blankets to wear when the cold winds cover our mother, the earth."

The girl was surprised and blushed. She had always dreamed of weaving a blanket for a chief. "Great Spirit," she prayed, "please guide my hands to make a blanket worthy of this great chief."

Early the next morning, Mockingbird Song and Flower After the Rain journeyed to a nearby canyon to look for a special plant. Mockingbird Song hadn't walked this trail in a long time. Because of her health, the old woman rarely traveled far from the hogan. Often of late, it was Flower After the Rain who gathered the wood and the corn and tended the sheep.

But today was a special occasion, so Mockingbird Song shuffled her weary feet over the desert floor. "Granddaughter," she said, "yesterday the chief told me he wants a yellow as bright as Grandfather Sun in his blanket. There is a plant that grows here that I have used to dye wool this color."

While searching for the plant, Mockingbird Song tripped on a rock and fell to the hard red earth. Flower After the Rain rushed to help her grandmother. But Mockingbird Song, proud as she was old, said, "Leave me be, child. There is nothing I can't do myself."

Flower After the Rain turned away. Tears streamed down her face. She was frustrated that her grandmother refused her help.

After Mockingbird Song stood up, she pointed to a rabbitbrush plant that grew on the floor of the canyon. Flower After the Rain reached to pick some leaves from the bush. In her excitement, she forgot to pray. Mockingbird Song gently reminded the girl by saying, "Granddaughter, before you take anything from the earth, you ask permission from Great Spirit, the Creator of all things."

Flower After the Rain looked up at the sky. She then reached down and patted the earth with both hands, touching it as a child touches her mother. The girl took a deep breath as she looked all around.

"Great Spirit," she said, "I look in the four directions—east, south, west, and north—and I see the beauty that surrounds me. I see the canyon walls, the clouds, the sky, the cornstalk, and the sagebrush. You, Great Spirit, have made all these things, and I am grateful. May I use this plant in my work?" Flower After the Rain felt a warm breeze caress her hair as she collected the plant's leaves.

On the way back to the hogan, Mockingbird Song needed to rest again. So as they passed their cornfield, she led Flower After the Rain into the middle. "Granddaughter," the old woman said, touching a cornstalk, "the earth is wise. She teaches us about giving and receiving. Look at this corn plant, which grows from a small seed stretching to touch Father Sky. Her roots reach deep into the soil to be nurtured by Mother Earth. Her stalk is heavy with corn. And before we pick the sacred corn, we offer prayers of gratitude because she gives her harvest to feed our people. Then, from the corn, we gather more seeds to begin the cycle again. There is a balance to all things, granddaughter, and giving and receiving are part of that balance."

When they returned from their walk, Flower After the Rain began to doubt her skills. She had always dreamed of making a blanket for a chief. Now she worried if her blanket would be good enough.

When Mockingbird Song saw the girl's expression, she held her close and said, "Granddaughter, your hands make blankets of great beauty. Trust yourself, child, and always ask Great Spirit to guide you."

During the following days, Flower After
the Rain wove the chief's blanket with much joy.
And at night, while coyotes sang to the moon,
Mockingbird Song wove stories of her life and her
meetings with the great chiefs from the north. Even
though they were happy, Flower After the Rain
never forgot about her grandmother's ailing body.

One morning, the girl ran into the hogan and said, "Grandmother, the sheep are ready to take down to the river."

But Mockingbird Song was still in bed. "Grandchild," she said, "I am not well today. I will stay here until you return."

"If you are ill," the girl replied, "then I will ask the medicine man to sing a healing chant for you."

"No!" Mockingbird Song said. "I will be strong tomorrow."

Reluctantly, Flower After the Rain left to do the chores. She was sad because her grandmother refused her help again. Down by the river, the girl let her mind drift and was soothed by the sound of the water. The spirit of the river consoled her, and as she grew peaceful, an idea came to her. Upon returning to the hogan, Flower After the Rain worked feverishly to complete the chief's blanket.

The girl awoke early the next morning. She stood in front of their hogan, scattered corn pollen on the cool desert sand, and prayed to Great Spirit.

Then Flower After the Rain folded the beautiful chief's blanket and stole off to look for Pinto Horse Man. She found him in the canyon watering his horses and told him her plan. Soon afterward, Flower After the Rain was on her way back home. When she arrived, the girl was relieved to find Mockingbird Song gone. Quickly, Flower After the Rain sat down in front of the hogan and began to plan for a second chief's blanket.

When the old woman returned, weary from her chore, Flower After the Rain greeted her with a smile and said, "Grandmother, close your eyes. I have a surprise for you."

Mockingbird Song rested her aching body on the good red earth. Sitting with eyes closed, she held out her hands and expected Flower After the Rain to hand her the finished blanket. Instead, Mockingbird Song heard the whinny of a horse. The aged weaver opened her eyes. She saw Flower After the Rain standing next to two beautiful horses whose coats were as golden as the sun.

Suddenly the old woman realized what her granddaughter had done. She felt anger rising in her stomach, like a hot ball of fire. Mockingbird Song faced Flower After the Rain with a look as hard as stone and said, "Granddaughter, you traded the chief's blanket for horses. How could you do this?"

Flower After the Rain looked out across the desert. She was frightened of her grandmother's anger, but she stood tall and said, "Grandmother, you have taught me the wisdom of Mother Earth— the teaching of giving and receiving. Today I give this horse to you. She is my gift to ease your journey."

The old woman gazed into her granddaughter's eyes. She saw how much the child loved her. Mockingbird Song's anger melted away, and she said, "Thank you, granddaughter. I am honored to receive your gift."

"Tomorrow, Flower After the Rain, we must take the horses down to the canyon and pick more rabbitbrush plant for the chief's blanket. And this time, I will ride like the wind."

"Yes, Grandmother," said Flower After the Rain. "Tomorrow I will begin weaving my second chief's blanket."

A Brief History of the Navajo Chief's Blanket

Between 1820 and 1880, Navajo weavers living in what is now the Four Corners region of the American Southwest produced the popular Navajo blanket, a body of art that ranks among the finest aesthetic accomplishments of the nineteenth century. These Navajo women were dedicated, inspired artists who supported their families and enhanced the material wealth of their tribe by weaving blankets of incomparable beauty and value.

The most recognizable style of the nineteenth-century Navajo blankets was the chief's blanket. It was considered a "man's shoulder blanket," was woven as early as 1800, and became a prestige garment among Plains Indians—Arapaho, Cheyenne, Sioux, and Ute tribes. The term *chief's blanket* grew out of the fact that high-ranking members of the Plains tribes were the only Indians who could afford to trade for and keep such valuable garments.

In the mid-1800s, to accommodate American Army personnel and American settlers who were moving into the region, trading posts sprang up throughout the area. Some traders befriended the Navajo people, learned their language, and helped design and market the chief's blanket to these new "customers." Hence, during this time the trading post became an integral part of the life of the weaver.

In the past 150 years, the Navajo people have witnessed many profound changes to their lifestyle. They have endured many hardships. However, in the face of all these changes, the Navajo tradition of weaving has withstood the test of time because today, over a century later, the women continue to produce their finely woven blankets and rugs.

In writing *The Chief's Blanket,* an important consideration was to accurately portray the nineteenth-century Navajo people and their culture. In pursuit of this goal, I received invaluable support from Pearl Sunrise and Joshua Baer. Pearl Sunrise is an award-winning Navajo weaver and Navajo cultural historian. Joshua Baer is the managing partner of Joshua Baer & Company, a fine arts gallery specializing in classic American Indian art. It is with deepest gratitude that I extend my thanks for their time and assistance.

—*Michael Chanin*